Out of Bounds!

"What's this kid doing here?" a tall boy with buzzed blond hair asked.

"He's my brother," Frank answered.

"We don't want younger kids on the team," the boy snapped. "And he can't even skate."

"My dad said he can be on the team, Darren," Chet said, moving over close to Joe. "And my dad's the coach."

"We're going to lose all our games if we have a team full of wimpy little kids," Darren growled.

"I'm not a wimp," Joe said at the same time as Frank said, "He's not a wimp."

"Then go play on another team," Chet said to Darren.

"I've been skating at this rink since I was three," Darren said. "I'm staying. And that kid better not get in my way!"

The Hardy Boys® are: The Clues Brothers™

Available from MINSTREL Books

The Hardy Boys® are:

THE CLUES BROTHERS™

15

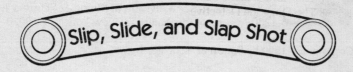

Slip, Slide, and Slap Shot

Franklin W. Dixon

**Illustrated by
Marcy Ramsey**

A
MINSTREL®
BOOK

Published by POCKET BOOKS
New York   London   Toronto   Sydney   Tokyo   Singapore

This book is a work of fiction. Names, characters, places and incidents are products of the author's imagination or are used fictitiously. Any resemblance to actual events or locales or persons living or dead is entirely coincidental.

A MINSTREL PAPERBACK *Original*

 A Minstrel Book published by
POCKET BOOKS, a division of Simon & Schuster Inc.
1230 Avenue of the Americas, New York, NY 10020

Copyright © 1999 by Simon & Schuster Inc.

ISBN: 0-671-03254-2

First Minstrel Books printing October 1999

10 9 8 7 6 5 4 3 2 1

THE HARDY BOYS® ARE: THE CLUES BROTHERS is a trademark of Simon & Schuster Inc.

THE HARDY BOYS, A MINSTREL BOOK and colophon are registered trademarks of Simon & Schuster Inc.

Cover art by Thompson Brothers/Bruce Eagle

Printed in the U.S.A.

PHX/

1

Slap Shot Superman

"Hey, Mom, Dad, guess what?" Frank Hardy burst in through the kitchen door. A big gust of wind swept in with him. It sent napkins swirling off the table his brother, Joe, was just setting for dinner.

"Hey, watch it!" Joe yelled. He grabbed at the napkins.

"Whoa there, tornado!" Mr. Hardy looked up from tossing the salad. "Where's the fire?"

"Dad—you'll never believe this," Frank began.

Mr. Hardy held up his hand. "You don't have to yell, Frank. We're right here in the same room."

"Sorry, but it's such great news."

"Then don't just stand there—tell us!" Joe yelled as loudly as Frank had.

Frank grinned. "Chet's dad is going to coach a hockey team—real ice hockey. He used to play hockey when he was in college. So can I sign up? The first practice is tomorrow night."

Mrs. Hardy looked across at her husband. "I don't see why not," she said.

"I think it's a good idea," Mr. Hardy agreed. "You boys should play some kind of winter sport. I don't like it when you're stuck in the house. And hockey is fun."

"Me, too?" Joe asked. "If Frank's going to play hockey, I want to also."

"I don't know, Joe." Frank frowned. "Only fourth graders are on the team. It might be kind of rough for you."

"Hey, I'm tough. I can take anything you can take. Right, Dad?" Joe stared Frank straight in the eye.

"But you don't know how to skate," Frank said.

"I do, too. Remember we went skating last winter?"

"Once," Frank said. "And you spent most of the time sitting down."

"I'm a quick learner," Joe said. "And you don't know how to skate any better than me."

"I do so," Frank said. "I've been practicing with Chet's in-line skates. They're almost the same as ice skates."

"Only not as cold when you fall down," Joe added.

"I think Joe should give it a try if he wants to," Mrs. Hardy said.

Mr. Hardy nodded. "I agree. Skating builds strong legs and quick reflexes."

"Just the things a detective needs, right, Dad?" Joe asked.

Mr. Hardy smiled. "Okay, we'll call Mr. Morton to ask him if you can join the team with Frank."

"Thanks, Dad." Joe grinned at Frank.

"You'd better not complain if the fourth graders are too rough for you, Joe," Frank said.

"I don't complain when I play football with your friends, do I?"

"Nooo . . . ," Frank had to agree, "but ice hockey is a tough sport."

"They have strict rules for hockey for younger players," Mr. Hardy said. "No contact allowed. I started playing when I was about your age."

"You were a hockey player, Dad?" Frank asked.

"You bet. I played all the way through high school. I wasn't bad either. I'll try to make it to some of your practices. Maybe I can give you some pointers."

"Can you teach us how to do a slap shot, Dad?" Joe asked.

"Sure I can," Mr. Hardy said. "I used to be known as the slap shot superman—and try saying that five times quickly."

"Slap shot superman," the boys yelled together. Then they started laughing.

"This is going to be so cool!" Joe said.

"Yeah, real cool. Especially when you're sitting on the ice, Joe." Frank gave his brother a friendly punch on the arm.

Joe couldn't wait to go to the rink for the first practice the next day. He dreamed about hockey that night. In his dream he glided over the ice with no effort.

"Joe, sit still please," Mrs. Hardy said as she drove them to their first practice. "I can't see in my rearview mirror because you keep jumping up and down."

"I can't wait to get there!" Joe said. "I bet I'm going to be a hockey whiz."

"Some whiz. You couldn't even stand up last time," Frank said. Then he dodged as Joe went to punch him.

"I'm driving you tonight because I have to sign you up for skate rentals," Mrs. Hardy said. "But from now on you can ride with Chet."

"Yeah! We get to ride with Chet," Frank said happily. Chet was his best friend at Bayport Elementary School.

When they got their rental skates Joe tried not to show that he was disappointed. The boots were old and beat up. When he put them on they felt wobbly and not very comfortable.

Joe began to have second thoughts. He remembered how hard it had been to balance on skates. He remembered how hard the ice had been when he'd fallen down on it!

"Come on, Joe. The other guys are already

out there," Frank called from the locker room door. "Do you want me to give you a hand?"

"It's okay. I can do it," Joe called back.

Joe staggered out after Frank. Frank seemed to walk easily on the thin blades. The other boys were already on the ice. Joe recognized Peter and Mark and Jose from Frank's class. They were right in the middle of the rink, a long way from the barrier. They all looked as if they knew how to skate.

For a second Joe thought about telling Mr. Morton he didn't want to join the team after all. But then he knew he wasn't going to quit in front of Frank and the fourth graders.

Chet clomped over to them. He was munching on Cheezy Wheels, his latest favorite snack.

"Hi, Joe. I didn't know you could skate," he said.

"Sure I can," Joe said at the same time Frank said, "He can't."

"It's been a long time since I skated." Joe glared at Frank, telling him to shut up. "I'll remember as soon as I get out on the ice."

"Chet, I thought I said no snacks at the rink!"

Mr. Morton called from the ice. "Go throw them away right now. We don't want crumbs on the ice. They might make someone trip."

Chet made a face. "I haven't finished my Cheezy Wheels. How am I going to skate with no energy?" he muttered to Frank and Joe.

Frank grinned at Joe. "When it comes to food or skating, Chet will always choose food," he said. "Come on, Joe. Let's get out there. Do you want a hand?"

"I can manage," Joe said. "You don't have to treat me like a little kid."

"Okay, suit yourself," Frank said. He stepped onto the ice and skated out to the other boys. Chet followed him.

Joe took a deep breath and stepped onto the ice. "Ready or not, here I come!" he yelled.

Joe tried to skate like the hockey players he'd seen on TV, but suddenly his legs were going in different directions. He couldn't control them at all. His ankles were wobbling like crazy.

"Whoa!" he yelled. He came flying into the group of boys and grabbed onto Frank to stop himself.

"What's this kid doing here?" a tall boy with buzzed blond hair asked.

"He's my brother," Frank answered.

"We don't want little kids on the team," the boy snapped. "And he can't even skate."

"My dad said he can be on the team, Darren," Chet said, moving over close to Joe. "And my dad's the coach."

"We're going to lose all our games if we have a team full of wimpy little kids," Darren growled.

"I'm not a wimp," Joe said at the same time as Frank said, "He's not a wimp."

"If you don't like it, go play on another team, Darren," Chet said.

"I've been skating at this rink since I was three," Darren said. "I'm staying, but that kid better not get in my way."

He skated away really fast and sent up a shower of ice when he stopped. Joe wished he could do that.

"Don't mind him," Chet said. "He thinks he's so hot. You'll be fine, Joe."

"I will be when I can make my feet obey me," Joe said.

"You'll get the hang of it," Chet said. "Come on, Frank. Take his arm. We'll skate him around a bit."

Joe linked arms with Chet and Frank. They started to skate with Joe in the middle. Slowly Joe got the feel of pushing forward with one skate, then the other.

"See? You're doing better already," Chet said. "Now try it on your own."

He gave Joe a push. Joe felt himself gliding over the ice. "Hey, I'm doing it!" he yelled.

Just then someone came shooting past him like a mini tornado. Joe only had a second to realize that the skater was Chet's little sister, Iola. The next second he had lost his balance.

"Whoa!" Joe yelled. His feet went flying and *bam*—he sat down hard on the cold ice.

He looked up when he heard giggles. Two girls were standing on the other side of the barrier, watching him. They were dressed in matching red skating outfits and white tights. They had matching ponytails, only one was blond and one was brunette.

With a sinking feeling, Joe recognized one of the girls. Over her red outfit, the brown-haired girl was wearing a white fake fur jacket with a hood. She had white skating boots slung over her shoulder. She was Melissa Jonas from his third-grade class. At school she was always a pain and a snob. Now Melissa leaned over and whispered to the girl beside her.

Joe tried to get to his feet, but his feet kept slipping away from him.

The girls were still laughing. The blond girl was laughing really loud.

"Boy, what a loser," she said. Her voice echoed across the ice. "That guy looks like his legs are made of spaghetti!"

Joe closed his eyes. He wished he could sink through the ice and disappear. How was he ever going to face Melissa at school again? How was he going to show her that he wasn't a loser with spaghetti legs?

2

Danger: Flying Puck

The next day at school Joe tried to stay away from Melissa Jonas. He just hoped that she wouldn't say anything about his skating disaster. But he knew she'd probably blab to the whole class.

Sure enough, Melissa was looking around for him when she came into the classroom.

"Hi, Joe," she said sweetly. "Does it hurt to sit down this morning?" Then she giggled.

"Why should it hurt to sit down?" Joe's friend Mike Mendez asked.

"Because I fell down on the ice at hockey

practice yesterday," Joe said quickly, before Melissa could say anything.

"You're doing ice hockey now?" one of the other boys asked. "I thought you had to be in fourth grade to do that."

"They're letting me play on my big brother's team," Joe said.

"Letting you play?" Melissa spluttered into her hand. "You can't even stand up on skates."

"I'm just learning," Joe said. "I bet you couldn't stand up the first time you tried."

"It was so long ago, I can't remember," Melissa said. She tossed back her long, dark hair. "I started skating when I was four. I've already been in hundreds of competitions."

"Wow, Melissa, are you going to the Olympics someday?" Tina Gonzales asked.

"It's my dream," Melissa said. "But it's going to be really, really hard. There are so many good skaters."

"Are you the best at your rink?" Tina asked.

"One of the best," Melissa said.

"I'd love to see you skate," Tina said.

Melissa made a face. "We've got a big meet

coming up this weekend, and guess what? Now we've got to share the ice during some of our practice time with a bunch of dweebs on a hockey team. It's not fair. How can we practice our routines when they're taking up half the ice?"

"Our hockey team might be going to the Olympics some day," Joe said.

Melissa gave a high, phony giggle again. "Oh yeah, right. Fat chance," she said.

Joe decided that he was going to learn to skate really, really well, just so that he could show Melissa she was wrong.

That afternoon Joe put his skates on quickly and was out on the ice, practicing before any of the girls arrived. His legs already felt stronger.

"Hey, you're getting the hang of it, Joe," Frank said.

Iola skated past. "Yeah, Joe. Let's see you do this!" She stretched one leg out behind her.

"How come your sister can do stuff like that?" Frank asked Chet as he came out onto the ice.

14

"She joined the skating club this year. She's getting pretty good, isn't she?"

Iola skated back to them. "Not as good as Jamie and Melissa," she said. "They are so awesome. I wish I could skate like them."

Joe looked across the ice. The girls from the skating club had just arrived.

"Which one is Jamie?" Joe asked.

"See the two girls in the matching red outfits? They always dress alike. The one with the blond hair is Jamie." Iola pointed to the girl who had made fun of Joe. "She's the best. She's going to the Olympics someday."

"What about Melissa?" Joe asked.

"She's really good, too—almost as good as Jamie. As good as I'm going to be someday."

Iola skated away to join the girls at the other end of the rink. She made skating look so easy. Joe gritted his teeth. If Iola could do it, so could he.

He watched as Jamie and Melissa skated out onto the ice. Jamie glared in his direction. Her voice carried clearly across the ice. "Oh no. Don't tell me those hockey creeps are here again. How are we supposed to practice when we have only half the rink?"

"How are we supposed to play hockey when half the rink is full of dumb girls?" Darren yelled back.

"Yeah!" Peter and Mark agreed.

"You don't have a big meet coming up this weekend," Jamie said. "And you're just beginners. It's not fair."

"If you don't like it, go somewhere else, Jamie Farley," Darren yelled again. "Good riddance."

"Just ignore him, Jamie." Melissa slipped her arm through Jamie's and pulled her away.

Coach Morton blew the whistle, and the boys started practicing drills. They had to skate across the rink, stop, turn, and skate back as fast as they could.

Darren did it perfectly. So did Chet and Peter. Frank was almost as good. At last it was Joe's turn. He skated out onto the ice. His legs felt stronger. He was going really fast. Cold air was rushing in his face. He felt great. He'd show those girls!

I'm doing it! he wanted to yell.

He tried to turn his skates sideways to come to a stop, but somehow his feet wouldn't turn. He just kept on going, out into the middle of the ice.

Suddenly something red flashed in front of him. It was Jamie. Joe felt his stomach turn over as they were about to collide, but Jamie pulled up just in time.

"You idiot!" she yelled. "You just messed up my routine. You're supposed to stay on your half of the ice."

"Sorry," Joe muttered. "I couldn't stop."

"Now I'll have to start over," Jamie snapped. "You guys are the biggest pain."

She skated off before Joe could say anything else. He skated back to the rest of the hockey team. His cheeks were burning.

"Don't mind her," Chet said kindly. "She's a spoiled brat."

Coach Morton called them over. "Now we're going to start passing drills," he said. "Get your sticks."

"Can I go to the bathroom first?" Chet asked.

"Hurry up then," his father said.

Chet skated off the ice. Joe made it to the

barrier and grabbed his stick. He lined up opposite Frank. They had to skate forward, passing the puck to each other as they went. Darren and Peter did it really well. Mark and Jose went next, but they still hadn't learned to skate and pass at the same time. They had to keep stopping to steady the puck.

Then it was Joe and Frank's turn. Joe tried extra hard. "The famous Joe Hardy slap shot!" he said to himself. He whacked the puck as hard as he could.

But the puck went sailing past Frank, right across the rink. It flew toward Jamie, just as she was landing from a jump. Joe closed his eyes. "Oh no," he muttered.

"Ow!" Jamie screamed.

The other skaters clustered around her.

"Are you okay? What happened?" Melissa asked.

"Something hit me on the leg," Jamie said.

"It was a hockey puck. Look, here it is." One of the girls bent to pick it up.

"Are you hurt, Jamie?" Melissa asked. "Do you think you'll be okay to skate on Saturday?"

"I don't know, It hurts a lot," Jamie said. She rubbed her leg where the puck had hit her. "I hope it's okay."

"We'll put some ice on it, just in case," her coach said. "Come on, let's take care of it right away."

"Those dumb guys are dangerous. I want them out of here," Jamie yelled, glaring at the hockey players.

"You wouldn't have gotten hit if you'd stayed on your half of the ice!" Darren yelled back. "You were on our half."

"So? I have to practice my routine, don't I?" Jamie demanded. "I'm going to get my dad to talk to the rink manager. It's not fair that we have to share."

Joe was feeling very bad. He watched Jamie go and sit down. He knew she was a brat, but he hadn't meant to hit her. He hoped his unlucky shot hadn't really hurt her leg and that she'd be able to skate on Saturday.

He kept looking over in her direction. He saw her sitting down with an ice pack on her leg. As soon as practice was finished he skated over to her.

"I'm really sorry I hit you with the puck," he said. "I hope your leg's all right."

"I guess," she said, looking away.

"I hope you're okay to skate at your big meet on Saturday," Joe said. "You're an awesome skater."

"Thanks," Jamie muttered. She looked up and gave Joe a little smile.

Joe felt better as he rode home with the Mortons. Maybe Jamie wasn't so bad after all. She was probably nervous about the meet on Saturday.

He realized that he was starving.

"Skating sure gives me an appetite," he said to Frank.

"Me, too," Frank said. "I hope Mom has dinner ready when we get home."

They came in to find their mother taking a dish of macaroni and cheese from the oven. It smelled wonderful.

"I can eat all that by myself," Joe said, grinning at Frank. "I don't know what Frank's going to eat."

"I thought that was all for me!" Frank answered.

They fought to get to the table first.

They had taken only a few bites when the phone rang. Frank answered it, then handed it to Joe. "It's your girlfriend," he teased.

"What?" Joe demanded. He took the cordless phone into the next room. "Hello?" he asked cautiously.

"Okay, you creep. Give it back!" a girl's voice shouted.

"Who is this?" Joe asked.

"It's Jamie from the skating rink, and I want my good-luck charm back right now!"

3

Clues Brothers—Seal Hunters!

Joe stood staring into the phone. "What are you talking about?" he asked Jamie.

"You know very well what I'm talking about. My good-luck charm. You took it!"

"Your good-luck charm? I didn't even know you had a good-luck charm."

"Sammy, my fluffy white seal," Jamie said. "He goes everywhere with me. He was in my bag on my seat when I started practice. You came to talk to me, and then he was gone. You took him to get even, didn't you? Just because I made fun of you and got mad at you."

"I didn't touch any fluffy white seals," Joe said angrily.

"It had to be you. Who else could it have been?"

"Well, it wasn't me," Joe said. "I wouldn't do a mean thing like that, even if you were a brat and laughed at me."

"Then where can Sammy be?" Jamie sounded as if she was crying now.

"Did you check under the seats?"

"I looked everywhere," Jamie said. "I looked under the seats, between the seats, in the locker room, and Sammy wasn't anywhere."

"Well, I didn't take your seal," Joe said.

"What am I going to do?" Jamie's voice sounded shaky. "I can't skate without him."

Suddenly Joe saw a way of showing Jamie that he wasn't totally clueless. "Don't worry. The Clues Brothers will solve this for you," he said.

"What are you talking about? What Clues Brothers?"

"My brother and I are great at solving mysteries," Joe said proudly. "Our dad's a real detective, you know. He's shown us how he solves cases. If you give me the facts, we'll find your good-luck charm for you."

"Would you really? That would be great. I really need your help. Sammy goes everywhere with me. I know I'd mess up if I didn't have him."

Joe thought this was pretty stupid, but he didn't say so.

"Okay, give me a description of, uh, Sammy," Joe said.

"He's really cute. He has soft, real-looking white fur and big, dark eyes. He's adorable—"

"Yeah, you already mentioned that." Joe made a face. "How big is it—I mean, he?"

"He's about as big as—as my teddy bear. Maybe about a foot long?"

"So, too big for someone to put in a pocket?" Joe asked.

"Unless it was a really big pocket," Jamie said.

"And you searched everywhere?"

"Everywhere," Jamie said. "And my friends helped me look, too. We even looked in everyone's bags, just in case Sammy got in

one of them by mistake. And we searched the lockers in the locker room."

"Can you think of anyone who might have taken Sammy to spite you—besides me?" Joe asked.

"It *had* to be one of you hockey players," Jamie said. "Who else could it be? You guys have been really rude to us. I just know it was someone on your team."

"I don't see how," Joe said. "We were all down at the other end of the rink."

"Then who?" Jamie's voice wobbled again as if she was about to start crying.

"Don't worry," Joe said. "I'll talk to my brother about it. We'll figure out who took your seal and get it back to you."

"If only you really can, you'll save my life," Jamie said. "I'm counting on you, Joe."

"Sure. No problem." Joe's face felt hot as he clicked off the phone.

"What was that about?" Frank asked. He had come to look for Joe.

"It was Jamie from the ice rink. She thought I'd taken her good-luck charm."

"Her good-luck charm?"

"Yeah—some fluffy stuffed toy that she takes everywhere with her." He grinned at Frank. "She's lost it, and she thinks I took it."

"Why would you do that?"

"To get even because she made fun of me," Joe said. "I told her I wouldn't do a mean thing like that. She's really upset about it, Frank."

"So?" Frank said.

"I sort of told her that we'd find it for her," Joe said.

"You what?" Frank yelled.

"Don't blow your top," Joe said. "I told her we were famous detectives and we'd find her toy for her."

"Are you crazy?" Frank said. "What did you do that for?"

"She called me a loser. I thought I'd show her I could do things, too. She can skate. I can solve mysteries."

"Thanks for counting me in on this!" Frank complained. "How do you think we're going to find her dumb toy? If someone wanted to steal it, they could easily have slipped out of the rink with it. We'll never find it."

"It shouldn't be that hard," Joe said. "There was nobody at the rink except the employees, the girls from the skating club, and our hockey team."

"Correct," Frank said. "So where was this good-luck charm?"

"In Jamie's bag, on a seat beside the ice."

"And the only people around were the other girls and her coach," Frank said.

"But the other girls are her friends," Joe said. "Remember how they all came to help her when I hit her with the puck? They wouldn't do a mean thing like take her special toy. And she said they all searched their bags and the locker room."

"Well, there was nobody else," Frank said. "We stayed down at our end of the rink, and then we went straight to the guys' locker room . . ." He paused and frowned, as if he was trying to remember something.

"What is it?" Joe asked.

Frank shook his head. "Nah. That can't be right," he said.

"What?" Joe demanded.

"I saw Chet go down there in the middle of

practice," Frank said. "Remember he asked to go to the bathroom? Well, the guys' locker room is at our end of the rink. I looked up and saw him behind the seats at the other end. He was hurrying as if he didn't want to be seen. So what was he doing down there?"

4

Checking on Chet

Joe stared at Frank. "I can't believe that Chet would take Jamie's good-luck charm. Maybe he went to the other end of the rink to talk to his sister."

"Iola was out on the ice. I saw her," Frank said. "I can't believe that Chet would do something like that either, but he did stick up for you when Jamie laughed at you."

Joe nodded. "So maybe he was just trying to get even and teach her a lesson."

"The only way we'll find out is to go to his house and ask him," Frank said. He and Joe went back to the table, where Mr. and Mrs. Hardy were eating.

"Mom, Dad, may we go to Chet's house for a moment?" Frank asked.

"But you haven't finished your dinner," Mrs. Hardy said, "and it's almost dark."

"It's really important, Mom," Joe begged. "It will only take a moment. We have to ask Chet something, to help us solve a mystery."

"You and your mysteries." Mrs. Hardy shook her head, smiling at her husband. "I know where they get it from."

"Go on then," Mr. Hardy said. "But come straight back. We don't allow you out after dark, remember."

Iola opened the door when Frank and Joe knocked.

"We're eating dinner," she said.

"We just need to talk to Chet for a moment," Frank said.

"Come on in, then." Iola started to walk back into the kitchen.

"We need to talk to Chet out here," Joe said. "It's kind of private."

Iola grinned. "You think you'll get Chet to leave food to talk to you? Fat chance."

Frank and Joe followed Iola into the kitchen.

"Frank and Joe need to talk to you, Chet," Iola announced.

Chet looked up from a plate piled high with fried chicken, corn, and mashed potatoes. "Later, okay, guys? Can't you see I'm busy?"

"Hi, Mr. and Mrs. Morton," Frank said. "Sorry to interrupt your dinner, but we just need to ask Chet an important question."

"We need you to help us solve a mystery, Chet," Joe added.

"Mysteries are great, but dinner is greater," Chet said. "This is the most important part of my day! Can't you talk to me while I eat?"

"It's kind of private," Joe said. "It will only take a second."

Chet sighed and got up. "Okay. But it better be good."

"Oh, it's good all right," Frank said. He looked at Joe. Chet didn't seem too worried.

They went out into the front hall.

"Jamie's good-luck charm is missing," Joe said.

"Is that it? Is that what you dragged me away from fried chicken to tell me?" Chet made a face and looked back at the kitchen. "I know about it already. Iola told me. She said Jamie made a big fuss and made all the girls search their bags. Girls are so dumb—crying over a stupid stuffed toy! Anyway, serves her right for being so mean to you."

"She thought I took it," Joe said. "I know she's a pain, but I feel bad for her."

"But what's it got to do with us? What are you going to do—buy her a new toy?" Chet demanded.

"Joe told her we'd find out who took it," Frank said. "We thought you might be able to help us."

"Usually I love helping you with your mysteries," Chet said. "But this one's impossible. Anyone at the rink could have taken the toy and sneaked out with it. What are you going to do—search the whole of Bayport?"

"We thought you might know something about it, Chet," Frank said.

"Me? What would I know about it?"

"I saw you down at that end of the rink. You were hurrying behind the seats. What were you doing down there?" Frank asked.

Chet glanced into the kitchen, where the rest of his family was still eating. "Nothing," he said quickly. "I was just coming back from the bathroom. And I didn't go all the way to the other end of the rink."

Frank opened his mouth to say "I saw you" again, but then he shut it. Why was Chet acting so nervous?

"And anyway," Chet went on, "why would I have taken her dumb good-luck charm?"

"We thought you might have wanted to pay her back for being mean to Joe," Frank said. Joe nodded.

Chet shook his head. "That's stupid. I wouldn't waste my time. And you know that I couldn't have taken the mascot. You rode home in my car. Did you see me carrying a fluffy toy?"

"You might have stuffed it into your jacket," Joe said.

"You guys were right beside me when I put on my jacket. Besides, that jacket is too tight for me. I'd never have zipped it up with me *and* a toy in it."

Frank looked at Joe.

"You're right," Joe said. "We would have noticed if you'd left the rink with a fluffy white seal under your arm."

"All the guys would have noticed." Chet grinned. "They would have given me a hard time."

"That's true," Frank agreed. "Thanks anyway, Chet. Now you can get back to your dinner."

"Hey, you know what, though?" Chet stopped suddenly. "I know who did go down to that end of the rink. I passed Darren heading that way when I was coming back from—from the bathroom. What was he doing down there?"

"Darren?" Frank and Joe said at the same time.

"He was really mad at those figure skaters," Frank said slowly. "He thought it wasn't fair that we had to share the ice with them. Maybe taking the stuffed toy was his way of getting back at them."

"And he said he'd been coming to the rink for years," Joe added. "He would probably know how important Jamie's good-luck charm was to her."

"And he's probably mean enough to do it," Chet finished for them.

"Do you think your dad has Darren's phone number?" Frank asked.

"Sure. He has a team roster with all the phone numbers on it," Chet said. "I'll go ask him."

"Frank can call," Joe said. "Darren thinks I don't belong on the team."

"But he stood up for you when Jamie made a fuss," Frank pointed out.

"Yeah, that was weird," Joe said.

Chet came back with the team roster and handed Frank the phone. Frank dialed, then held the receiver so that Chet and Joe could listen.

"Hi, Hardy. What do you want?" Darren asked. He even sounded rude on the phone.

Frank told him about Jamie's missing good-luck charm.

Darren started laughing. "A stuffed toy? You think I'd really want my own fluffy, cuddly seal?"

"No," Frank said. "But we thought you

might have taken it to let the girls know you didn't want them sharing your ice."

"They already know that," Darren said. "I've told them enough times. How would taking a toy help?"

"Because Jamie thinks she won't skate well in the meet without it."

"That's baloney," Darren said.

"We're just trying to talk to everyone who went anywhere near Jamie," Frank said. "You went down to that end of the rink. You might have seen something."

"I went to use the pay phone at the snack bar," Darren said. "I suddenly remembered that I was getting a ride home with Peter. I'd forgotten to tell my mom not to come to get me. So I had to go call her. Coach Morton said I could."

"And you didn't see anyone go near Jamie's bag?"

"I didn't even look," Darren said. "Why would I care if anyone was near her bag? I just wanted to get back to practice."

"Okay, thanks, Darren," Frank said. "See you tomorrow."

He shook his head as he clicked off the phone. "Did you hear what he said? He has a good reason for being at that end of the rink. He was calling his mom from the pay phone. He said your dad gave him permission, Chet."

"That's easy enough to check out," Chet said. "And I saw him leaving after hockey practice. He had his skates over his shoulder and no bag. He had nowhere to put a toy."

"Could he have stuffed it into a skate?" Frank asked.

Joe shook his head. "It was too big. Jamie said it was about the size of a teddy bear. That wouldn't fit in a skate."

"He could have hidden it somewhere before he left," Frank suggested.

Suddenly Joe's face lit up. "Wait. I know where someone could have put the toy and nobody would ever notice it!"

5

The Cheezy Wheel Clue

Mr. Morton came out into the hall. "What's going on, boys?" he asked.

"Dad, at practice today did Darren ask you if he could go and call his mom?" Chet asked.

"Yes, he did. Why, what is this about?"

"One of the girls on the figure-skating team had her stuffed toy seal stolen," Frank said. "It's her good-luck charm. She thinks one of the boys on the hockey team took it. We were just trying to check who went down to that end of the rink during practice."

Mr. Morton frowned. "I hope one of my team wouldn't do a mean thing like that."

"We're trying to find out who really took the toy," Joe said. "And I just had a great idea where someone could hide a white fluffy toy— in that big pile of ice that the Zamboni machine swept up. You would never notice a white toy in the middle of all that white ice!"

"Great idea, Joe," Frank said. "Maybe the toy is still there."

"Let's go and look right now," Joe said. "Do you want to come with us, Chet?"

"Thanks, but I'd rather finish my meal," Chet said.

"I think we should all go, Chet," Mr. Morton said. "I want our hockey team to be welcome at the rink, not accused of stealing. I'll drive, but call your folks first, Frank. They might not want you out this late."

Frank dialed home.

"I don't know about this, boys," Mr. Hardy said. "It's a school night. What about home-work?"

"We'll do it, I promise," Frank said. "But it's very important we get back to the rink before they get rid of the ice in the corner. We think Jamie's toy could be hidden in it."

"Okay. I don't suppose I should stop two detectives in the middle of a case," Mr. Hardy said.

"Thanks, Dad. We won't be long, I promise," Frank said. "And Mr. Morton will drop us off on the way home."

"I really don't want to come," Chet said. "You guys are the detectives. You solve the crime, okay?"

"Get your jacket, Chet," Mr. Morton said.

Iola walked out of the kitchen. "I'm coming, too," she said firmly. She took her own jacket out of the hall closet. "I've got sharp eyes, and I can go in the girls' locker room."

"Good thinking, Iola," Mr. Morton said. He led the boys out the front door to the car. Chet was very quiet all the way to the rink.

When they got to the rink it was closed. The evening session of public skating didn't start until seven-thirty. Mr. Morton rang a bell next to the door. A worker at the rink let them in.

"The first place to check is the Lost and Found," Mr. Morton said. But the toy wasn't there.

"Has anyone cleaned up since our kids were here?" Mr. Morton asked the worker.

"The Zamboni has been out on the ice, but the seats and the locker rooms aren't cleaned until the morning," the man told them.

"Great," Joe said. "So if someone hid the good-luck charm, it's still there. Let's get started."

He ran straight to the pile of ice. The pile was bigger now, because the Zamboni had been around the rink again. The boys dug into the ice until their hands were turning blue.

"Nothing here but ice," Frank said. "And I feel as if my hands are about to drop off."

"Mine, too," Joe said. "My idea was good, but it wasn't right. But there are other places where someone could have stuffed a stuffed toy." He laughed. "A stuffed toy, get it?"

"This is a waste of time. Let's go home," Chet grumbled.

Frank looked at him. Chet wasn't usually grouchy. He clearly didn't want to be there. Could he know something about the missing toy after all?

"Okay, guys, let's search the locker room," Mr. Morton said.

"And I can search the girls' locker room again," Iola said. "Although Jamie made us search every inch this afternoon."

The Hardys, Chet, and Mr. Morton went through the guys' locker room. There were a couple of odd socks on the floor and one old sneaker in the corner, but not much else. When they came out, Iola was waiting for them.

"Nothing," Frank said. "How about you, Iola?"

Iola shook her head. "Nothing," she said. "But then some of the lockers had locks on them, so I couldn't see what was inside."

"There are still plenty of places to check out," Mr. Morton said. "Trash bins, under seats . . . It would be easy to hide a toy here."

"And we can look for clues, too," Joe said to Frank. "Maybe the thief left some kind of clue behind."

"This is stupid," Chet muttered, "and my dinner is now cold."

For the next half hour they went around the whole rink, looking under seats and in trash bins.

"Where was Jamie sitting?" Mr. Morton asked.

"Right about . . . here." Joe showed him. "Yes, look," he said excitedly. "This must have been her seat. There's something that looks like white fur caught on the rough edge of the seat. That could be some of Sammy's fur."

"Wait, there's a barrette on the floor here." Frank pounced on it. "Red, with two hearts on it." He held it out to Joe.

Joe backed away. "Don't give it to me. I don't want the cooties," he said.

"It's a clue," Frank said.

Iola laughed. "No, it's not. Jamie always wears those barrettes—they match her outfit. She must have dropped it herself."

Frank put the barrette in his pocket. He went on looking behind the seats. Suddenly he nudged Joe.

"Look, over here," he whispered. He bent and picked up something from the floor right behind Jamie's seat.

Joe examined it. "It's a chip," he said.

"A Cheezy Wheel. Don't you remember that Chet was eating them before practice?"

Joe looked around. Chet was standing at the other end of the rink, waiting impatiently.

"Don't you think that Chet is acting weird tonight?" Frank whispered.

"Yeah," Joe agreed. "He didn't want us to come back to the rink."

"And he wasn't telling us the whole truth," Frank said. "He said he didn't go down to this end of the rink, but I saw him. And now we've got the chip to prove it. If he didn't take the toy, what was he doing down here?"

6

Dancing Sickness

I can't believe that Chet would take a stuffed toy," Frank said. "It's just not like him."

"Then why didn't he want us to come back to the rink tonight?" Joe asked. "And what about the Cheezy Wheel on the floor. Nobody loves Cheezy Wheels as much as Chet."

"We'll have to talk to him when his dad's not around," Frank said. "He's our friend. I don't want to get him in trouble."

"Okay, let's go on searching." Joe sighed. "Maybe we'll find more clues."

They looked in every trash bin. They went

outside and looked around. But they didn't find anything.

"Maybe the toy got tossed into the Dumpster," Iola said. "I'll climb in and check for you."

"Iola, get back here," Mr. Morton called. "That Dumpster is too tall for a child to even lift the lid. And anyway, I watched all of my players get into their cars. Nobody went around the back of the building."

"See, I told you this was a waste of time," Chet said. He looked happier now. "Let's get out of here. Fried chicken is calling me!"

"I'll have to call Jamie when I get home," Joe said. "I hate to tell her that we haven't found Sammy yet."

"We'll just have to question everybody at practice tomorrow," Frank said. "Maybe someone saw something that will turn out to be important."

"I'm going to talk to Melissa in the morning," Joe said. "She's Jamie's best friend. She might have noticed somebody hanging around Jamie's bag."

But when Joe got to school in the morning, Melissa wasn't there.

"Where's Melissa?" he asked.

"Melissa is sick today, Joe," his teacher, Mrs. Adair, told him. Then she spoke to the class. "I have a favor to ask. Melissa's mother called to say that she was staying home today. But she'd like someone to bring her homework to her. Would someone volunteer to do that?"

Joe raised his hand. "I will, Mrs. Adair," he said. "I live only four houses away from her."

"Thank you, Joe," Mrs. Adair said.

Joe grinned. Now he had an excuse to question Melissa.

After school he met Frank, Chet, and Iola. They walked home together.

"Hey, slow down," Frank complained. "You guys are in such a hurry."

"I have a bag of Cheezy Wheels waiting for me," Chet said. "All afternoon with no snack is torture for me."

Joe looked at Frank and dug him in the side.

"Did you ask him yet?" he whispered.

"Ask me what?" Chet asked.

"Chet, there's something we need to know," Frank said. "You said you went to the bathroom at the ice rink. But the guys' bathroom isn't anywhere near Jamie's seat. I saw you down there, and we found a Cheezy Wheel right behind Jamie's seat. What were you doing down there if you didn't take Jamie's toy?"

Chet looked around, then beckoned Frank closer. "If you really must know," he whispered, "I was going to the snack bar."

"The snack bar?" Joe blurted out.

Chet put his finger to his lips. "Shhh. Don't let Iola hear, or she'll blab to my dad. He told me no snacks during practice. But I was starving. I asked to go to the bathroom, then I sprinted down to the snack bar, finished the Cheezy Wheels I had and got another bag."

"That's it?" Frank started to laugh.

"Of course. You believe me, don't you? If I had to choose between a stuffed toy and Cheezy Wheels, which do you think I'd go for?"

"The Cheezy Wheels of course," Frank and Joe said together.

"I don't think you'll ever find that toy," Chet said. "It's long gone."

"Don't say that," Joe said. "I told Jamie we were great detectives. Someone must have seen something. I'm going to talk to her friend Melissa when I drop off her homework."

"How come you got stuck with it?" Frank asked.

"I volunteered to take it, because we live so close," Joe said.

Frank looked surprised. "You said she was a snobby pain."

"I know, but I get to ask her questions about what she saw at the rink. She might give us a clue."

"Face it, guys," Chet said. "You're never going to solve this mystery. Someone walked off with Jamie's toy seal, and now it's gone. You can't search every house in Bayport."

"I'm still going to keep trying," Joe said. "The Clues Brothers never quit a case."

"I think I'd better come to Melissa's with you," Frank said. "Two detectives are better than one."

The Hardys left Chet and Iola at their front gate and walked on to Melissa's house. Loud music was thumping from inside the house. As Frank and Joe came nearer they saw someone dancing behind partly closed drapes. It was Melissa!

"She sure doesn't look sick to me," Frank said.

The moment they rang the doorbell the music stopped.

They waited and waited. Joe was just about to ring again when a weak voice said, "Who is it?"

"It's Joe Hardy and my brother, Frank. We've got your homework," Joe called.

The front door opened. Melissa was standing there, wearing a fluffy pink robe. She looked very pale and sick.

"Oh, Joe, Frank," she said in a croaky voice. "I'm sorry I took so long. My mom just popped out to the store to get me some throat lozenges. It took me a while to get out of bed—I'm feeling so weak and dizzy."

Frank and Joe sneaked a glance at each other. Then they stepped inside.

"I'm sorry to hear you're feeling so bad, Melissa," Joe said. "I guess that puts you out of the skating competition."

"I'm going to try to skate on Saturday anyway," Melissa said. "I've trained so hard for it. I thought I might get better if I stayed home today and rested." She held out her hand. "Thanks for bringing me my homework."

"No problem," Joe said. "I hope Jamie can skate on Saturday."

"Jamie?" Melissa asked. "Why shouldn't Jamie skate? She's not sick, too, is she?"

"No, but she's very upset about her good-luck charm. We searched and searched, but we couldn't find it. Jamie says she can't skate without it."

"I know. I helped her look," Melissa said. "Poor Jamie. She really believes that stuffed seal brings her luck. I don't know who could have taken it."

"We wondered if you might have seen something," Frank said.

"Like what?" Melissa asked.

"I don't know—anything unusual. Someone

hanging around her bag, someone who shouldn't have been in your part of the rink?"

"I did see that guy Chet go past once," Melissa said. "But I was working too hard at my skating to notice anything else."

"And you helped Jamie look in the locker room, too?" Joe asked.

Melissa nodded. "We went through everyone's bag. We looked in everyone's locker. I can't think what could have happened to Sammy. Poor Jamie."

"She'll probably skate just fine without him," Frank said. "She's a really good skater. I've watched her."

"But she really believes that Sammy helps her skate well. She's had him since she was five years old," Melissa said. She hugged the homework papers to her. "I have to go back to bed. My mom will be mad if she finds out I got up. Thanks again, Joe. I might see you at school tomorrow if I feel okay."

The Hardys didn't say anything until they were out on the sidewalk.

"So, what do you think?" Frank asked Joe as they headed for their own house. "She looked sick when she came to the door, didn't she—but we saw her dancing."

"I guess she wasn't feeling too great this morning," Joe said. "She decided to stay home to rest up for the big competition. Maybe her favorite song came on the radio and she just had to dance to it."

"Remind yourself never to take another case with girls in it," Frank said. "Guy mysteries are easy to solve. Girls are impossible!"

"We can't give up, Frank," Joe said. "We just have to think who wanted Jamie to lose. When we go to the rink we'll keep our eyes open. Maybe someone will be watching Jamie to see how she's skating today."

Frank nodded. "It's our only chance, I guess," he said.

Joe was thinking about what he could tell Jamie when he saw her at the rink. He didn't want to admit that the Clues Brothers hadn't a clue this time. He saw Jamie's face light up when she came speeding across the ice to him.

"Have you found Sammy yet?" she asked.

Joe shook his head. "Not yet, but we're working on it."

Jamie's face fell. "Okay. Thanks for trying," she said.

She skated away. She tried a jump and fell down.

The other girls watched her. "Poor Jamie," one of them said. "I feel so bad for her."

"I think this meet is jinxed," another girl said. "First Jamie's good-luck charm disappears, and then Melissa gets sick. Our two best skaters!"

"Is Melissa as good as Jamie?" Joe asked.

The girls nodded. "Almost," one of them said. "She's really good. Too bad she's sick. Now we'll never win the meet."

Joe heard Mr. Morton calling his hockey players. He made his way back across the rink.

"Okay, today we're going to try our first real scrimmage," Mr. Morton said. "We've got a practice game planned two weeks from now. I want you to start working together as a team. Hockey is all teamwork. Okay, let's have Darren, Frank, Freddy, Mark, and Joe on one team and the rest of you on the other."

Joe was excited to be playing in a real scrimmage. He skated across the ice on the left wing, ready for Darren to shoot him the puck.

Out of the corner of his eye he saw Jamie. She tried another jump and fell again. There was something about her. Joe stared hard, trying to think what it was. Suddenly he knew—Jamie was wearing two barrettes with hearts on them. Either she had more than one pair or the barrette they had found on the floor belonged to someone else.

7

All Seal-ed Up

Joe, that pass was meant for you. Pay attention," Mr. Morton yelled.

"How did you miss, Joe?" Frank asked. "That was an easy one."

"Sorry. I've got something else on my mind," Joe said. "I have an idea who took Sammy."

"You do? Who?"

"Get back on defense, you two," Coach Morton yelled.

"I'll tell you later," Joe said. He skated down the rink.

When the scrimmage was over, Jamie had gone.

"So what's your idea, Joe?" Frank asked.

Joe looked around. Chet and Iola were standing nearby.

"When we get home," he said, almost whispering. "I have to prove that I'm right before Iola blabs to everybody."

Frank sat impatiently in the car all the way home. As soon as Coach Morton let them out of the car, Joe grabbed Frank's arm.

"We have to go to Melissa's house," he said, dragging him down the block.

"Melissa? What for?"

"I think she can tell us something important," Joe said.

"Like what?"

"Like whether she lost a barrette and whether she's faking being sick."

"Why would she fake being sick?" Frank asked.

Joe grinned. "That's what we're going to find out."

They knocked on Melissa's front door. Melissa's mother opened it.

"I'm sorry. Melissa's sick," her mother said. "I'm afraid she can't have visitors."

"But this is very important, Mrs. Jonas," Frank said. "It will only take a moment."

"All right. But only a moment. She needs to rest up for the big meet."

Mrs. Jonas showed the Hardys into the family room. "Don't stay long and make her tired," she said. "I'm just fixing her dinner."

Melissa was sitting on the sofa with a blanket around her. She looked scared when she saw Frank and Joe. "What do you guys want?" she asked.

"I think we found your barrette, Melissa," Joe said. "The one with red hearts on it."

"You came over here to give me a barrette?" Melissa said.

"And I think we know who took Jamie's stuffed seal," Joe went on.

"You do? Who was it?"

Frank nodded. Now he understood what Joe was getting at. "Someone who dropped her barrette under Jamie's seat," Frank said.

"I don't know what you're talking about," Melissa said.

"We know why you stayed home today,"

Joe said. "You didn't want to go to practice and have to face Jamie."

"You're nuts," Melissa said.

"You were scared that you couldn't act normally in front of her," Joe said. "Then she'd realize that you took her good-luck charm."

"Me?" Melissa laughed. "Why would I take Sammy? Jamie's my best friend."

"So that you could win for once," Frank said. "The other girls said that you were a very good skater—almost as good as Jamie. But you always came in second. She was always first. That must have bugged you. You knew she wouldn't skate well without her good-luck charm, so you took it."

"But Jamie really is your friend. You didn't want to face her today, so you pretended to be sick," Joe added.

"That's baloney," Melissa said. "Ask my mom. I was really sick."

"Oh, right—so sick that you were dancing this afternoon. We saw you," Frank said.

"This is so crazy," Melissa said. "There was no way I could have taken Sammy. The skating team was together all the time when we searched everyone's bag and locker. How could I have taken Jamie's seal?"

"You probably got the idea when you put your coat next to Sammy," Joe went on. "Your white fur jacket matched Sammy's white fur. We found a tiny piece of white fur caught on the seat beside Jamie's."

"No wonder Sammy didn't show up in anyone's bag or locker," Frank said. "You had him hidden in your white fur coat, didn't you?"

"You can't prove anything," Melissa said angrily.

"No, you're right. We can't prove it," Joe said. "But is it really going to feel good if you win because Jamie doesn't skate her best?"

Melissa's lip trembled. A tear rolled down her cheek. "No, I guess not," she said. "It feels horrible. I wish I'd never taken the dumb thing."

8

The Slipping, Sliding, Slap Shot Star

Joe and Frank looked at Melissa as she sat hugging her knees.

"I really did feel terrible this morning," Melissa said. "That's why I stayed home from school. I felt sick to my stomach at what I'd done. How could I have done such a mean thing to my friend?"

Joe shrugged. "You didn't stop to think, I guess."

"You're right. I put my jacket down beside Jamie's bag. Her seal was poking out of the bag. It was made of the same fake fur as my jacket. Suddenly I got the idea. I took it and put it in my jacket hood."

"Oh, right. The jacket had a hood," Joe said.

Melissa nodded. "Sammy was totally invisible. I wore my jacket while we searched. Then I just walked out with the seal in my hood."

She reached under her blanket and hugged her knees closer. "As soon as I got Sammy home I felt bad. I knew I should call Jamie and tell her. But part of me really wanted to win, just once."

"To win by cheating?" Frank asked.

"You don't know what it's like, always being second-best," Melissa said. "Everyone calls Jamie the star and tells her she's going to the Olympics some day. I'm almost as good, but nobody says that to me. I'm just Jamie's friend." Melissa sighed. "I guess I should call her now and tell her what a bad friend I've been."

"I hope she understands," Frank said.

"So do I." Melissa got up from the couch. "I don't want to lose Jamie as a friend. I'm going to take Sammy back to her when I go to practice tonight."

"I'm glad I'm not a skating genius," Joe said to Frank as they walked home. "I wouldn't want to go through all that pressure."

Frank grinned. "I don't think you have anything to worry about."

"Unless I'm a hockey star someday."

"A hockey star?"

"I might be, someday, if I practice hard," Joe said.

"Right now your biggest worry is not sitting down too hard." Frank chuckled.

"Hey, you just wait," Joe said. "I have a feeling I'm going to be another slap shot superman, just like Dad."

"I'll believe it when I see it." Frank gave Joe a friendly push.

Two weeks later the hockey team had its first game. They had decided to call themselves the Bayport Barracudas. They were playing a team called the Grizzlies. The players looked like Grizzlies, too—big and mean.

Joe sat on the bench while the starters were on the ice. Darren scored a lucky goal. Chet was a great goalie and blocked a lot of shots. But the other Grizzlies were good skaters. They zoomed up and down the ice. Frank tried to block and got knocked over.

"Come out and rest for a while," Mr. Morton called to him. "Joe, go in for your brother."

Joe took a deep breath and skated out onto the ice. The Grizzlies took another shot. Chet blocked it and cleared it out to Joe.

Suddenly the puck was in front of Joe. He started skating with the puck toward the Grizzlies' goal. He saw one Grizzly coming at him, but he dodged him. Joe kept on going. The goal was in front of him. "Slap shot superman," he whispered to himself. He swiped at the puck with all his might. It sailed into the back of the net.

Joe couldn't believe it. He heard cheering as he skated back to his teammates.

"Way to go, Joe!" he heard his dad's deep voice boom out.

"Yeah, Joe! Way to go!" a high voice screamed. Jamie and Melissa were jumping

up and down on the sideline. They were best friends again.

Jamie had said she could understand how hard it was for Melissa to be second-best. Well, she didn't have to worry about that anymore. Melissa had won the meet. Jamie had come in second. Sometimes Joe wondered whether Jamie had let Melissa win. He would never understand girls in a million years!

Darren skated over to him. "Hey, Peewee, you're not so bad after all," he said. He slapped Joe on the back. Joe's feet slipped and he sat down hard. He slid across the rink and bumped into Frank. Frank bumped into Chet. Chet bumped into Peter. They all fell down.

Frank got up and held out his hand to Joe. "Hey, whose side are you on?" he asked.

"I just scored us a goal!" Joe said as he got to his feet. "I didn't know Darren was going to knock me halfway across the rink. Did you see my slap shot, Frank? It was awesome, wasn't it?"

"It sure was." Frank laughed. "So was that slide. My brother, the king of the slip, slide, and slap shot!"

The Hardy Boys® are:

THE CLUES BROTHERS™

By Franklin W. Dixon

Look for a brand-new story every other month

A MINSTREL® BOOK

Published by Pocket Books

1398-09

THE NANCY DREW NOTEBOOKS®

#1: THE SLUMBER PARTY SECRET 87945-6/$3.99
#2: THE LOST LOCKET 87946-4/$3.99
#3: THE SECRET SANTA 87947-2/$3.99
#4: BAD DAY FOR BALLET 87948-0/$3.99
#5: THE SOCCER SHOE CLUE 87949-9/$3.99
#6: THE ICE CREAM SCOOP 87950-2/$3.99
#7: TROUBLE AT CAMP TREEHOUSE 87951-0/$3.99
#8: THE BEST DETECTIVE 87952-9/$3.99
#9: THE THANKSGIVING SURPRISE 52707-X/$3.99
#10: NOT NICE ON ICE 52711-8/$3.99
#11: THE PEN PAL PUZZLE 53550-1/$3.99
#12: THE PUPPY PROBLEM 53551-X/$3.99
#13: THE WEDDING GIFT GOOF 53552-8/$3.99
#14: THE FUNNY FACE FIGHT 53553-6/$3.99
#15: THE CRAZY KEY CLUE 56859-0/$3.99
#16: THE SKI SLOPE MYSTERY 56860-4/$3.99
#17: WHOSE PET IS BEST? 56861-2/$3.99
#18: THE STOLEN UNICORN 56862-0/$3.99
#19: THE LEMONADE RAID 56863-9/$3.99
#20: HANNAH'S SECRET 56864-7/$3.99
#21: PRINCESS ON PARADE 00815-3/$3.99
#22: THE CLUE IN THE GLUE 00816-1/$3.99
#23: ALIEN IN THE CLASSROOM 00818-8/$3.99

by Carolyn Keene
Illustrated by Anthony Accardo

Simon & Schuster Mail Order Dept. BWB
200 Old Tappan Rd., Old Tappan, N.J. 07675

A MINSTREL BOOK
Published by Pocket Books

Please send me the books I have checked above. I am enclosing $_____ (please add $0.75 to cover the postage and handling for each order. Please add appropriate sales tax). Send check or money order--no cash or C.O.D.'s please. Allow up to six weeks for delivery. For purchase over $10.00 you may use VISA: card number, expiration date and customer signature must be included.

Name _____

Address _____

City _____ State/Zip _____

VISA Card # _____ Exp.Date _____

Signature _____ 1045-16

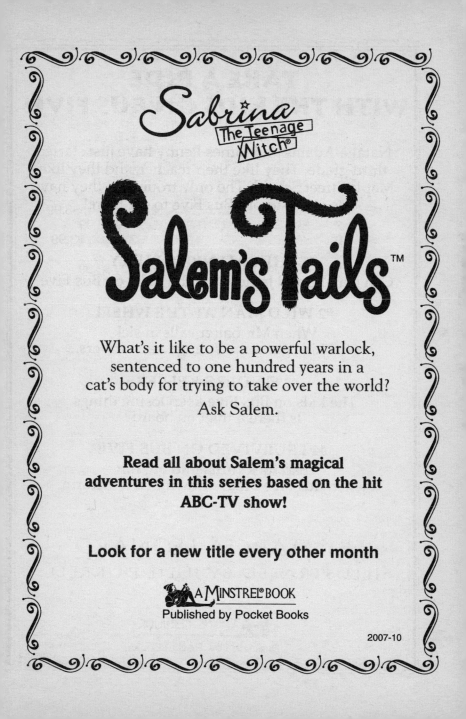

TAKE A RIDE
WITH THE KIDS ON BUS FIVE!

Natalie Adams and James Penny have just started
third grade. They like their teacher, and they like
Maple Street School. The only trouble is, they have
to ride bad old Bus Five to get there!

#1 THE BAD NEWS BULLY
Can Natalie and James stop the bully on Bus Five?

#2 WILD MAN AT THE WHEEL
When Mr. Balter calls in sick,
the kids get some strange new drivers.

#3 FINDERS KEEPERS
The kids on Bus Five keep losing things.
Is there a thief on board?

#4 I SURVIVED ON BUS FIVE
Bad luck turns into big fun
when Bus Five breaks down in a rainstorm.

BY MARCIA LEONARD
ILLUSTRATED BY JULIE DURRELL

A MINSTREL BOOK
Published by Pocket Books

1237-04